This Is the
FIREFIGHTER

by Laura Godwin
Pictures by Julian Hector

Disney • HYPERION BOOKS
New York

For James Fraser
—L. G.

For Pat Cummings
—J. H.

First Edition
1 3 5 7 9 10 8 6 4 2
Printed in Singapore
Reinforced binding
Library of Congress Cataloging-in-Publication Data on file.
ISBN 978-1-4231-0800-9
Visit www.hyperionbooksforchildren.com

This is the firefighter.
These are his clothes.

This is his truck,
and this is its hose.

This is the station.
This is the bell.

And this is the signal
that all is not well.

This is the squad car,
this is the street.
These are the flames,
and this is the heat.

This is the building
caught in the flurry.
This is Command, shouting,
"Bring the hose, hurry!"

This is the ax
that knocks down the door.

These are the people
who wait on the floor.

This is the wave.
This is the shout.

These are the firefighters
who bring each one out.

This is the ladder,
attached to the truck,
that reaches the lady and man
who are stuck.

This is the firefighter
who climbs through the heat.
These are the people
who wait in the street.

This is the rescue.
This is the cheer
that roars through the crowd
when the signal's "All clear."

This is the smoke
as it drifts far away.
This is the glow
at the end of the day.

This is the company—
Eight-fifty-zero.
This is the firefighter.
This is the hero.